# GOON BITCH

## My Number One Goon

By

*SOULJA CHOC*

*&*

*BLACK DIAMOND*

# Legal Notes

# Table of Contents

# SYNOPSIS

A tale of two rival crews fighting to be number one. For years, they had a mutual agreement not to cross paths with each other, until the leader of the Taylor Made Boys, Montez Santana was found murdered in God's territory, leaving his wife, Jewelz with questions in her mind, and revenge and malice in her heart.

On the other side of town, God is dealing with his own problems of mistrust and deception within his organization. With the stress of deceit, he decides to clear his head in his self-owned lounge where he meets a young lady that peaks his interest, but there is more to her than meets the eye.

With all hell breaking loose, will God find what he needs to know about his mystery woman in time to save her life? Will Jewelz find out the truth about her husband's death in the midst of trying to prevent her own?

# GOD

"You niggas can't do shit right!" I yelled as I stood behind the desk in my office. "What the fuck do I have to do, come out of retirement?" Three of my goons stood on the opposite side of my desk, and I stared each one of them in their faces. I was looking for a sign of weakness and the moment that I saw one, they would end up sleeping with the flowers.

"I always end up having to call a bitch to a do a man's job, but y'all wonder why she's riding around in a Bentley." I shook my head as I spoke because these niggas were always throwing salt on ole girl, but she always got the job done.

"She's sexy though, man. With an ass that big, she can walk up on any nigga she wants to, man. We can do it like her. We have to find sneak attacks and shit," Cee said as he looked directly at me. Any other time, I'd shoot a nigga in the kneecap for speaking out of turn, but I had respect for him.

"An excuse is like a lie, my nigga. Everybody got one to tell--some more than others. Don't tell me why you can't get shit done, man. Just find a way to get it done! The hard part is out the way. Lil' Choc Gotty is performing tonight, get there by 11:30 so you can catch him before he leaves. Can y'all handle that?" I asked silently, wishing a nigga would tell me something I didn't want to hear to give me a reason to shoot him.

"Yea, we got this, big homie," Lito said right when Cee opened his mouth to respond. I nodded my head then dapped them up. That was their cue to get on down, so I walked over to the door and let them out.

As they walked out of the room, Cee's older sister walked in. I sucked my teeth as I eyed her shape. She had my weed and cigar ready for me to roll up, so I took it from her then sat down on the couch.

This bitch was always ready and had my dick out and in her mouth before I had time to break my weed down. Her mouth was so wet that it took me a minute to focus on the task at hand. "Hold on real quick, ma," I said to her so I could at least get the weed in the cigar without dropping it, but she didn't listen.

I licked the cigar as she slid her tongue up and down the shaft of my dick. I took a deep breath then filled the cigar up, rolled it up, then ran the blunt over the lighter. I could feel her throat muscles clench my dick as she bobbed her head up and down.

I lit the blunt then hit it as my free hand gripped the back of her head. She was deep throating my shit effortlessly; she had a nigga questioning himself and shit. I was legit sitting there trying to figure out if this bitch had a throat or if my shit just wasn't as big as I thought it was.

I began to pump into her mouth, and she met me halfway with each stroke as I stared on in disbelief. There was no way in hell this bitch was doing me like this. She gripped my dick with one hand and began to massage up and down with the same rotation as her mouth.

I leaned my head back as she cupped my balls in her hand massaging them as she sucked harder and faster. I could feel my nut rising instantly after that, so I gave her mouth three more short pumps then yanked her head away just in time to nut all over her face.

I expected her to have an attitude or something for nutting on her face, but she began to lick my now semi hard dick until there was no nut in sight, then stood up to her feet and headed for the bathroom. I knew she was about to wash her face, but I hoped she was about to brush her teeth as well.

I stuck my dick back down in my boxers, then zipped my pants up. *Now that the nut is out of the way, it's time to get to work,* I thought to myself as I grabbed a duffle bag from the side of the couch then dumped the cash on the table.

Coco, Cee's older sister walked out of the bathroom ready to work as well. "Go grab the money machine," I said to her, then waited for her to bring it to me. Once she came back with it, I placed the money inside of the machine to be counted. By the time I finished running the money through the money machine, it came out to be a total of one-hundred thousand dollars.

I let Coco leave, then called up my right-hand man, No Good so he could pick the money up then take it the safe house. It didn't take him but about fifteen minutes to pull into my driveway, so I walked out of my office and met him in the front of my house.

By the time that he made it to the door, I already had it unlocked, so he was able to walk right on in. "What's good, my nigga?" he asked as he gave me dap.

"Ain't shit, my nigga, just tryin' to put this shit together," I answered honestly as my eyes scanned my living room. I wasn't looking for anything in particular, but I did like to be completely aware of my surroundings at all times.

"So, you really goin' step back and let me run shit?" he asked as he rubbed his hands together. I could tell he was excited about my offer even though he had no idea why I was letting him make this move.

"Yea man, it's your time to shine. I'm just going to run the business side of things," I said to him, when in all actuality, I was done taking penitentiary chances. I'd rather be on the business side of things and keep my freedom.

"I already know, and you know what you need, my nigga. I got you!" he said, and I dapped him up again then handed him the bag.

"It's one hundred racks in the bag. Drop it off at the spot then meet me at the lounge. I'll have more details for you then," I said to him, and he nodded his head.

"Yeah, I have some things to run by you anyways, so I'll wait till we meet up then to fill you in," he said.

We both got up and walked out the house together. He hopped in his Bentley, and I hopped in my Maserati, and we backed out of my driveway. It took me twenty minutes to get to the lounge, and since I owned it, I was able to park out front.

I was greeted by some of my employees as I walked in and headed straight for my designated table. Most of them were happy to see me, but I didn't miss the nasty looks that Cheryl was giving me because I refused to give her anymore of this dick because she couldn't handle it.

See, Cheryl started working here about six months ago, and the bitch was throwing the pussy at me before she had a clue who I was. Now, I normally wouldn't mix business with pleasure, but a few months later, she caught me slipping. I was tipsy, and we fucked. Shit was supposed to be just that simple, but she couldn't handle the dick.

I wanted to fuck with her a little bit, so I winked at her as I sat down at my table and waited for No Good to show up, but she just rolled her eyes and walked off. No Good and I went way back to those sand box days, so you could safely assume that we grew up together. We handled everything together until we started pulling in major ducks.

At that point, I knew that we needed to chill out and let other people take those risks so we could chill out. The only problem was that No Good enjoyed taking those risks, but he was far too sloppy and brought our organization far too much heat, so it took some major convincing to get him to see it my way.

He finally arrived about fifteen minutes later and headed straight to my table, so I waved a waitress over and we got down to business. "You ready for this, my nigga?" I asked, and he nodded his head.

"You already know," he answered amped up. "I was born to do this gangsta shit," he continued, and I just leaned back and smiled.

"That we were, my nigga. That we were," I spoke as I sat up then leaned my frame on top of the table. "It'll be a fairly easy transition because you already know the ins and outs of the business. I'll call a meeting Friday and let the lieutenants know they'll be reporting directly to you from now on," I explained.

"Bet! That's what's up. The only thing I'm going to change is I'm not gonna be as easy on these mother fuckers as you've been. They goin' have to come correct or be dealt with accordingly," he spat, but I didn't have anything against any of his plans unless it was going to cause me to lose money.

"Like I said, you goin' be running it, so do it how you do. Just remember what I said back when we started ringing bells in these streets. Not every action needs a reaction. Be calculated with it." I had to break it down for him so it would forever be broken.

"Now that we got that shit out the way, here's what I wanted to holla at you about. One of the lieutenants from the east side came up short the last two times. So, do you want it handled your way or do you want it done my way?" No Good laid it out for me.

"Since we haven't announced the change just yet to the lieutenants, I'll get at him tomorrow, but after the meeting, it will be all on you to make that decision," I informed him.

"You right, you right. But I was going to make an example out of his ass and let them boys know what will happen if the thought crossed their mind to play with money or work," he said, and I could tell that this power was going to go to his head quickly. I just hoped that he didn't get himself killed.

"Well, now that you broke it down like that, how about you tag along with me tomorrow and we both handle it?" I said so I could see for myself how he would really get down if he was the boss before now.

# JEWELZ SANTANA A.K.A. TAMEKA TAYLOR

After working a double shift at the hospital, I was beyond tired and ready to get home. My walk-in shower and Cali King sized bed were both calling my name, but I also couldn't wait to be wrapped in my husband, Montez's arms.

I walked into the employee parking lot, hit the button on the key ring to start my engine, then climbed inside of my all white Beamer with a peanut butter interior. Hearing the soft purr of my engine caused an immediate smile to spread across my face because I absolutely loved my car.

Although I was a nurse that made pretty good money, I was able to live this luxurious life because of my husband. He went out of his way to make sure I didn't need or want for anything, and I'd always love him for that.

As I pulled off into traffic, Lyrica Anderson's smooth voice came out of the speakers as she sang her new single "Don't Take it Personal." It took me thirty minutes to drive home, and I was in deep thought the entire time.

The first thing I noticed after pulling in my driveway was Montez's new Land Rover parked in the circular driveway of our mini mansion. *Damn, my baby is making major moves at just twenty-eight,* I thought to myself as I got out of the car a proud wife.

I walked inside of our quiet home then kicked my shoes off at the door. I knew he was asleep, and I also knew that I wasn't too far behind him. I headed straight to our room, grabbed what I was sleeping in, then headed to the bathroom.

Our shower was large with multiple shower heads and a glass door enclosing it--another luxury I insisted on. I turned on all four heads and let them hit my tired body from all angles. I picked up my loofah and squeezed my Victoria's Secret Love Spell body wash on it and lathered my body from top to bottom leaving no spots unattended. Ten minutes later, I got out drying my body and looking myself over in the mirror.

*Yeah, my body is on point!* I thought as I applied lotion to my 5'7", 160-pound frame. My breasts were perky, my ass sat up just right, and my stomach was flat enough to surf on. My caramel complexion and hazel eyes gave me a certain exotic appeal that made every man that had ever crossed my path mouth water.

I slipped on my boy shorts and my cami, then went to join my husband in our bed. I know I was knocked out before my head hit the pillow good.

After a couple of hours of sleep, I heard Soulja boy's "Flick of The Wrist" blaring through my once peaceful sleep. *Oh God, not now*, I thought as I tried to tune it out, but it continued to ring until Montez answered it in his sexy, sleepy voice.

"What it do, my nigga?" I heard him mumble sounding just as aggravated as me. I wasn't asleep all the way anymore, so I just laid there with my eyes closed. "What?" he raised his voice an octave. "The fuck you mean, man?" he yelled, then the covers flew completely off of me.

I opened my eyes then climbed out of the bed so I could pick our cover up off of the floor. "Ain't no way that shit ain't at the spot, bruh! Man, Jewelz is going to nut up on my ass. I just got back this morning!" I could hear Montez snapping out, and even though I didn't know exactly what was wrong, I knew it was bad. "Alright Montana, come scoop me up. I'm getting dressed," he spat angrily, and I sat down on the edge of our bed.

I had a funny feeling in the pit of my stomach because I knew that something wasn't right. I watched Montez walk in the closet then come back out with clothes in hands. "Babe, what's going on? Where are you going?" I needed to know what was going on, and I needed to know right then.

"Oh, good morning, babe." He walked over to me then planted a soft kiss on my lips. "Montana needs me to take a run with him real quick. I'll be back soon," he said as he finished getting dressed.

"Wait, why are you and Montana going? Don't you usually send someone else for stuff like this?" I asked nervously.

"Yeah, we do, but nobody else can handle this, and my dog said he needed me, you know I can't let him down as much as he has been there for us," Montez stated.

"Baby, don't be like that; you been helpin' me run this shit for years, so you know how the game go, and I don't trust nobody else when it comes to this amount of money and work," he said pulling me into his arms and kissing me gently. We had a chance to talk for a few minutes about what we were going to do when he finished handling this business before his cell phone started ringing again.

"I'm on the way out now," Montez answered.

I got up to walk him out, but I still couldn't shake this strange feeling I had. "Baby, be careful out there," I whined watching him check his gun and put it back in his waistband.

"Always, baby," he said before walking out of the door. I waved at Montana before closing the door behind him. I tried to lay back down and go to sleep, but it wasn't happening, so I picked up the phone and called my bestie, Gabrielle. I hoped she was off today because I didn't want to stay at home alone.

I let the phone ring three times before I got an answer. "What you doin', bitch?" I asked.

"Shit, nothing much, sitting at the house chilling with my sister, Pamela," she replied.

"Can y'all come over and keep me company? I don't want to be here by myself," I begged.

"Only if you got something to smoke and drink," Gabrielle stated.

"Girl, I got y'all, come on," I informed her before hanging up. Twenty minutes later, I heard the doorbell ring. "Come in!" I said through the intercom in the bedroom. I had finished putting on my white Seven jeans that hugged my body and blue baby tee showing off my navel ring. I slipped on my fuzzy footies since I didn't allow shoes on my carpet and walked to the living room to greet my company.

We had a great time together, and I really missed days like this, but I still couldn't keep my mind off of Montez.Once they went home my nerves was still all over the place, He'd been gone for hours and hadn't called me or answered his phone for me. I called him a few more times, and he still didn't answer. It was so strange because he always answered my calls. I was trying not to panic, so I made myself believe that he was in a dead zone and just wasn't getting any of my calls.

I pushed the bad thoughts to the back of my mind and went to watch TV for a while and wait on my husband so we could go somewhere like we planned. I must have fallen asleep because I woke up to the constant ringing and banging on the front door. I jumped up and ran to the front door. I didn't even ask who it was before swinging the door open.

"Jewelz, they killed him! They killed Montez!!" Montana shouted as he stood before me covered in blood and breathing heavily. He almost collapsed at the door, but I helped him inside the foyer and sat him in a nearby chair with my hands shaking and my heart racing.

"What the fuck happened? Who killed Montez?" I asked hysterical.

"It was an ambush. I tried to warn him, but it was too late. They shot him, and then they shot me," he blurted out. I was numb and in shock. *My husband, the love of my life is dead,* I thought to myself as I began to rock and cry.

"Jewelz! Help me!" Montana yelled, snapping me out of my trance. I ran to get my medical bag and treat the gunshot wound to his arm.

I removed his jacket causing him to whine in pain. I noticed that the bullet was lodged in his left bicep. I sterilized the wound before removing the bullet. I wasn't fully equipped at home, so I had to use some surgical scissors to dig the bullet out. Once I got it out and I was bandaging it up, the unthinkable happened. Montana grabbed me and kissed me. I pushed him away from me and continued to bandage him. "Montana, when I am finished, you need to leave my house."

"I'm sorry, Jewelz-- I didn't mean it. I just don't know what to do with myself without my Best friend and brother," Montana admitted.

"So, you just goin' try to fuck his wife? Come on, Montana, you need to go home and rest," I spoke harshly. I was devastated and didn't have time for no extra shit right now.

I had to get him out of here before the cops came, which I knew they would because my husband wasn't a nobody. He had ties to some very powerful people, a few I knew that the cops didn't even want to see.

Montana stood there looking at me like I was about to be his last supper giving me an eerie feeling. "Get out my house, dammit!" I screamed. I didn't know what it was, but shit wasn't adding up, and I needed to be alone to figure it out. I slammed the door behind him and slid down it crying because this couldn't be happening. I knew in this game things like this could happen, but I never thought I would be a widow at twenty-six-years-old.

A couple hours later, just like I suspected, the cops were at my door to tell me the news that my husband was dead. They asked if I could come down to the morgue and identify the body. I told them that I would be down as soon as I changed clothes and got myself together.

When I got down there and saw him, my heart damn near stopped. Seeing him lying on that cold table with no clothes on and bullet holes riddling his body, I fell to my knees in defeat. I couldn't take the pain of knowing the man that I loved, the man that had saved me from a horrible life, would never be beside me again. He would never hold me or tell me how much he loved me again.

The coroner helped me to my feet and to a chair outside the door where the cops were posted up asking me questions like, "Did he have any enemies, or was there anyone that was giving him problems?"

I simply shook my head no and asked them could I go home.

When I got home, I realized I didn't want to be alone, so I picked up the phone and called Montana. I was sure that he was hurting too, and I felt like shit for treating him so badly. He answered the phone on the first ring sounding more hurt than ever, so I invited him over so we could talk.

Thirty minutes later, the doorbell rang, so I drug myself out of bed to answer it. I already knew who it was, so I swung the door open without checking and fell into his arms. "I'm so sorry this happened," Montana said, causing me to think about Montez all over again. I just wanted to be close to him and to be held, so when he scooped me up and carried me to the couch, I didn't put up a fight.

I was hurting on the inside, and I felt like a piece of myself had died right along with my husband, so at this point, I just wanted to feel anything other than what I felt in that moment. I stared Montana in his eyes, but I envisioned Montez the whole time. He leaned closer to me and wiped the tears away as they slid down my cheeks.

His fingers brushed across my neck slightly, and an inviting moan slipped from my lips. I turned my head to the side, and he began to circle his finger softly in circles on my neck. I had my eyes closed, so when he leaned over and kissed me, it wasn't expected, but it was welcome.

Our kiss deepened, and when I opened my eyes, I saw an expression on Montana's face that I'd never seen before, but I ignored it. He pulled my shirt over my head, then took my nipple into his mouth hungrily.

I leaned my head back and moaned as I pinched the nipple that wasn't in his mouth. Tears continued to slide down my cheeks as he got up and laid my body flat on the couch. I looked down at him as he began to trail soft kisses down my stomach, then took my belly ring into his mouth.

He slid my boy shorts down my legs then tossed them across the room as he spread my legs. I was beginning to have second thoughts, but when his breath tickled my clit, all logic flew out of the window. I inhaled sharply as he sucked my clit into his mouth then eased his middle finger and ring finger deep in my pussy.

I began to wind my hips faster and faster because I could feel my orgasm building up, but I was having trouble cumming. He looked up at me with lust filled eyes. "Cum for me," he whispered harshly, then slipped his tongue in my ass without removing his middle finger and ring finger from my pussy. He sucked so hard on my clit while applying pressure to my G spot, and my body began to jerk uncontrollably.

My mouth opened wide, but no words came out as I came all over Montana's face. I'd never had a nut before that made me cry, but I cried harder than ever as I laid across the couch. The head obviously wasn't enough to fill the void of my missing husband, so I sat up with my tears steadily streaming down my cheeks and pulled his dick out of his pants.

He stood up quickly then pulled a condom out of his pocket and slid it down his massive dick. He gently pushed me back down onto the couch then eased into me slowly. I bit down on my bottom lip as he hissed like a snake. "Shit, Jewels!" he moaned as he began to stroke me slowly. "You so fuckin' tight and wet!" He closed his eyes as if he had to focus on something else.

I can't lie and say that I wasn't enjoying how he was making my body feel, but somehow, my mind wandered off to who could have killed my husband. I felt like shit for fucking Montana before my husband's body had even cooled off when I should have been hitting the streets trying to find the person responsible for my man's death.

I closed my eyes and imagined that it was Montez on top of me instead of Montana, and within minutes, we came at the same time. We both laid completely still, but I knew we weren't thinking about the same thing. I had questions, and I needed answers.

"Where was Montez killed?" I asked, then held my breath as I waited for an answer.

He looked at me with sorrow in his eyes, "Over in God's territory, Jewelz."

# GOD

I had a lot on my mind, so I was chilling at the lounge trying to clear my mind. Cheryl was aggravating the fuck out of me trying to get my attention by walking back and forth, but I refused to acknowledge her. I had more pressing issues to handle.

My phone began to vibrate in my pocket, and when I pulled it out, I saw that it was my Aunt Tiny calling. "What's up, Tiny?" I answered the phone as I stared down at the drink in front of me.

"Have you heard from Jap? He hasn't been answering my calls or texts." She sounded so stressed out, and I didn't blame her because one thing about Jap was he never missed a day without checking on his mom.

"Let me see what I can figure out, and I'll call you back," I said, then hung the phone up. I immediately called No Good. I knew that if Jap wasn't answering, then he more than likely missed her chemotherapy appointment, so I knew something had to be wrong.

"What's crackin', my nigga?" No Good asked as soon as he answered the phone.

"Aye, you seen Jap?" I asked as I began to tap my thumb against the table with a deep scowl on my face.

"Yea, 'bout two days ago," No Good responded cooly.

"Alright bet. When you slide through that side of town, stop by the spot to see if he there, then hit me back so I can let my aunt know what's up. She's looking for him," I stated because I felt a little better about this situation knowing that he'd been seen.

"Give me ten minutes, my nigga. I'm headed there now," he said, and we ended the call. I sat my phone on the table, and just as I looked up, I saw this sexy chick walking straight towards the bar. My phone vibrated because a chick that had I coming through to meet me at the club later was confirming, but I may have to cancel on her. I wasn't sure just yet, so I ignored the text message.

I looked back up, and the girl at the bar was ordering a drink. I got up and put my phone in my pocket and went to the bar and sat next to her. I looked over at her, and she turned her head the other way. I chuckled then looked at her and waited for her to turn her attention back towards the bar.

Cheryl had been watching me watch ole girl, so I knew that was the reason why she walked over to her. "Do you need anything else?" she asked her, but the woman shook her.

"I'm good for now," the woman responded, so Cheryl walked away but didn't walk away too far. I took that as my cue to spark up a conversation with the woman.

"How you doin', beautiful?" I asked as I stared directly at her.

"Fine, and yourself?" she responded. I examined her entire body from head to toe before I responded.

"I see that big ole rock on your hand. Where your husband at? Why you sittin' at the bar by yourself?" I questioned because I could sense some trouble at home.

"I'm a widow, and a man is the last thing on my mind," she responded coldly.

"Is it possible for me to get to know you?" I decided to shoot my shot anyway even though she'd just made it clear that she wasn't interested.

"No, it's not possible, and honestly, it has nothing to do with you. My husband hasn't been deceased a month yet, and honestly, if he was, I wouldn't be ready to date right now." She sounded so sad, so broken, but before I could respond to her, Cheryl resurfaced.

"Can you give me a double shot of Hennessey?" the woman asked as she handed Cheryl her credit card. My phone began to vibrate in my pocket, and when I saw that it was No Good, I walked away from the car to answer.

"Tell me something good, my nigga," I spoke precisely as soon as I answered the phone.

"Awe man, it's all bad, my nigga. Get over to the spot," No Good said, causing me to get a funny feeling in my stomach.

"What the fuck you mean it's all bad, Good?" I asked as I turned around so I could get ready to head straight there, but I needed to know what I was getting myself into first.

"Man, just come over to the spot, my nigga," he responded then hung the phone up. By the time I stuck the phone back down in my pocket, I noticed that the woman was gone, and Cheryl had made her way to the other end of the bar. I shook my head at her when she smirked at me, then headed to the spot.

It took me 20 minutes to get to the spot. When I pulled up, I got out and walked inside. It was the lieutenant who ran the spot, Dre, No Good, and a couple of the workers. As soon I walked in, No Good told the workers to step outside for a minute. Once they were outside, No Good looked at Dre and said, "Tell the homie what you just told me."

"He's gone, man," Dre said, and I cocked my head to the side.

"What the fuck you mean he gone?" I questioned.

"He was the one stealing the money, so I took care of it," Dre said.

"Nigga, you did what?" I said as I walked towards him. Before he could respond, No Good put his hand on my chest stopping me before I could lay my hands on him.

"Hold on, my nigga," No Good said, and it had me looking at him sideways.

"Man, you the one that told me it didn't matter who the fuck it was to kill them when I found out, so I did what you told me to do," Dre spoke up.

"Nigga, I didn't know it was my mutherfuckin' cousin!" I yelled. my heart went out to my aunt because I didn't think she could take much more.

"You the one that gave the order, my nigga," No Good said, and I couldn't even be mad at them because he was right. I'd ordered the death of my own blood.

"You right, my nigga. You right, man." Then I backed up. I took a few steps back. I was hurt and felt bad at the same time. Not only did we fuck Dre up and give him two black eyes, but we gave him the order to kill my cousin. Now I had to go home and tell his mama that he'd been killed.

I looked at Dre and said, "You right, lil' nigga, and I apologize for us putting our hands on you."

"It's all good, big homie. I understand," Dre said as he reached out and gave me some dap. "Y'all put me over this spot, and it was my job to make sure shit like that didn't happen."

“We both learned a valuable lesson from this situation, but I gotta go, man. I have to go talk to my auntie and let her know that her son won’t be coming home,” I said sadly as I shook my head.

“Aight, big homie.” I gave Dre dap and then gave No Good dap, and we embraced just before I left.

# MONTANA

It had been three weeks since we laid Montez to rest. I missed my nigga, and I felt bad as fuck for killing him, but in a way, it wasn't my fault. All he had to do was loan me the money I needed to pay my debts, but he refused.

I promised him I was going to pay it back as soon as I got back on my feet, but he had to start talking that self-righteous shit asking me what I be doing with my money because I made almost the same amount of money as him and Jewelz together, but didn't have nothing to show for it. Granted, if I wasn't high off cocaine and mollies at the time and in my feelings, I probably wouldn't have killed him, but friend or no friend, nobody talked down on me.

I remembered thinking back to the duffel bag filled with money and drugs in my trunk that we had just picked up, and that sealed his fate. I realized where we were at and that we shouldn't have been over there meeting on God's territory. I knew I could get away with it. I slammed on my brakes suddenly, telling him that something was wrong with the car. I stopped in the middle of what looked like a deserted street and pulled the lever to open my hood. I got out, and Montez followed to try and help me figure out what was going on.

I let him fiddle around and check different things under the hood, and when he raised his head to say that he didn't see anything wrong, I had my gun pointed in his face, and I let go five bullets in different parts of his body. I watched his body hit the ground shaking and convulsing. I heard the bloodcurdling sounds, and I knew his lungs were filling with blood with his eyes open staring at me. He held his arm up and mouthed for me to help him.

"You should have just given me the fucking money, nigga!" I yelled at his dead body before jumping back in my car and speeding off.

"Shit, Shit!" I yelled banging my hands on the steering wheel realizing I had fucked up and I needed to come up with a lie to tell Jewelz and the crew. I rushed towards the direction of their house, and once I got a few minutes away, I pulled over and shot myself in the bicep, but the bullet ended up grazing my side too. I remember how bad that shit hurt driving up to Montez's house to put on one of the biggest performances of my life.

But like the old saying goes, "All good things come to an end." My gambling debts and markers had racked up to well over a million dollars, and the Italians in Las Vegas were sending clear threats that my time to pay up was coming.

When I got home last night, I found my daughter's pit bull, Lady hanging in the hallway with her chest cut open and a note saying, "In two weeks, this will be you."

I had little to no money or drugs left; even the four-hundred thousand I had taken from Montez was gone because I went to Detroit to some other Casino to try and double it but ended up losing it, and now I owed them too. My plan was to pick up the money from Montez's dope houses and disappear, but as I was slowly finding out, Jewelz had changed up the operation and had LA pick up everything yesterday and bring it to her. So now I was I desperate and running out of options.

I had been wanting Jewelz since the day I met her at the club, but she was secretly with Montez already, and from the looks of it, she had no plans of leaving him alone. I said secretly because she was in an abusive relationship with a big-time nigga in Atlanta named Money. He was beating on her and making her sleep with me for money among a lot of other things.

Montez came up with a plan for us to get her away from him. He booked a date with her at an upscale hotel where we were waiting to take her to the airport and bring her back to California. By the time she got here, he had changed her name to Tameka Taylor and everything about her. He got her back in nursing school and gave her a new beginning.

I guess I didn't know my best friend as well as I thought I did, because I just knew if something ever happened to him, I would be the one to take over our operation and make sure his wife and family were taken care of because that's what we had discussed, but after the reading of the will, I was shocked and angered that he had left everything under Jewelz's control. Only twenty-thousand a piece to the crew including me. There was another envelope given to her that nobody knew what was in it. The lawyer said she was to read it when she was alone.

Sitting here in the Zaxby's restaurant, a sinister thought crossed my mind, and I wondered how much Money would pay to find out where his number one bitch was and how well off she was now. That nigga Money was a beast in the streets. Maybe if I put him on to her whereabouts, he would kill her, and I could really have the organization that I helped build.

# JEWELZ

I swear these last couple of weeks have been hell on my soul. I miss being held, talking and laughing with my husband, but he gave me everything he had to give in this world and left me with the key to his kingdom.

I'd been off for two weeks trying to get my life back together and handle Montez's business affairs. I had been watching his best friend, and the more I saw, the more I didn't trust him. I believe that he had something to do with Montez getting killed because I found out a couple of days ago that there was a price on his head for unpaid gambling debts.

I found out through LA, my husband's little brother, that Montez was starting to have doubts about Montana's loyalty to him and his organization. I'm pretty sure that Montana didn't know when he went in the gas station that day that Montez had called LA and told him that the deal Montana claimed he had set up, he had a bad feeling about it.

I told him that they had four-hundred thousand and four keys in the trunk of the car. Funny thing was, the night everything went down, Montana never said anything about no money or no work. When I questioned him about what they were doing that day, he told me they went to check one of the stash houses for some missing work.

That's what I remembered my husband saying on the phone that day. "Ain't no way that shit ain't there, man!" were his exact words. So, how was it that they ended up making a sale that big after product had just come up missing? Then, the order didn't come in until after they had made the weekly pickups from the trap houses. Third, how and when did he start doing business with God's people? Them niggas on the West side had damn good dope. It wasn't as pure as ours, but definitely high grade.

I got out of bed to get dressed for work with hella shit going through my head. Revenge being at the top of the list. My husband left me a letter with his will that I was told to read when I was alone. In the letter, he told me if anything happened to him, to remember everything he taught me; stay armed up, keep LA by my side, and be prepared for enemies known and unknown. I took his advice and changed the whole operation. I made LA my right-hand man and kept a team around my house and a few people down the street from my job.

I didn't know who this God person was yet, and my people were having a hard time finding out, so I guess it was going to be a job for me and my girls with our bodies, brains, and willingness to kill at the drop of a dime. We were definitely some Goon bitches.

If we couldn't get to him, we would just befriend his crew, and when I found out who was doing business with Montana and had a hand in killing my husband, I was going to paint this city red.

I grabbed my purse and walked out of the door. I saw LA, Derrill, and Creep on the front lawn talking and kicking the shit when I walked out to get in my car. I waved and turned my back to unlock the door.

"Get down!" I heard before I was knocked to the ground and gunfire erupted. I couldn't get to my gun because LA wouldn't let me move as he laid on my back busting both of his Glock 17's.

"Urrgh…I'm hit!" I heard before Creep fell down just a few yards away from me.

"Cover me!" Derrill yelled at LA trying to pull Creep out the line of fire. Juan and Dino opened the door of the house busting their guns while Derrill helped Creep in the house. LA got up and ran farther in the yard still firing with me hot on his heels with my .380 side by side. We fired without stopping as we heard the screeching tires speed off. I pulled out my phone and called 911 running back to the house.

I saw broken glass all on my porch and the bullet holes that riddled my beautiful home. I looked at LA shaking my head because he was hype pacing back and forth. "I'm going to kill them niggas, Jewelz. What the fuck they think this is?" he spat."

We will get them, bruh. Right now, we have to see about Creep and hide all the guns that are not registered," I told him with my adrenaline rushing.

I went in the house and collected the guns from the crew and hid them in the floor safe in my room. I came back out with clean towels, latex gloves, and a scalpel so I could get the bullets out and apply pressure to Creep's chest. I immediately jumped into action because he was struggling to breathe, and it wasn't looking good. He had two gunshot wounds--one to the chest and one to the stomach

"Shit!" I yelled because I didn't have what I needed to work on him here. "Lay him flat and apply pressure to the wound, or he is going to bleed out," I demanded.

I heard the sirens in the distance, but he was losing consciousness. A few minutes passed, and the medics came rushing through the door with the police right behind them. They were asking questions about what had happened, but I couldn't answer because my main concern was trying to save Creep. He was too young to die like this.

The medics tried to move me out the way, but I wasn't budging. I was trying to get the bullets out. "Ma'am, what are you doing?" the young white medic asked.

“I'm a nurse; I'm trying to save his life, dammit!” I screamed. They lifted him on the stretcher and started a line before loading him in the back of the ambulance.LA was still talking to the cops when I interrupted.

“LA drive my car to the hospital, I'm going in the ambulance with Creep. Derrill, Juan, and Dino stay here until Gabrielle and Pamela show up, then all of y'all come to my job,” I ordered and jumped in the ambulance.

They worked on him all the way to the hospital. I called ahead on the radio and told them to set up an OR room because he was going to need emergency surgery. It was a good thing I was a charge nurse at the hospital with a little pull, or he would have had to wait until they could set up a room.

It took fifteen minutes for us to arrive, but my coworkers were already outside waiting for him. I was a nervous wreck these boys were there to protect me, and now one was fighting for his life. I didn't know who was trying to kill me, but I was about to set this city on fire. I was supposed to be working, but I couldn't do my job in this condition, so I stayed by the nurse’s station in the OR room and waited.

A little while later, two more gunshot victims were brought in with a gang of niggas in tow. It was straight chaos in the small area with emotions running high. They were demanding answers about their friends. I did the best I could to help the nurses get some order when I noticed a familiar face staring at me. At first, I couldn't remember where I had seen him before, and then it hit me, he was the dude from the lounge a couple weeks ago. He had a stone cold look on his face, but when I smiled, it softened up a little. I wondered who this man was, but from my first impression, his demeanor screamed Boss.

# GOD

I stood in the lobby of the emergency room with my hands in my pockets. A member of my crew had been shot in the midst of trying to rob a bank--young people, I swear. I stared straight ahead at the woman that had come into my spot just a few short weeks ago. She looked like a boss as she walked around trying to calm everybody down, but they didn't know this was the calm before the storm.

I'd found out that not only had my cousin been stealing from me, but he'd been put down because of it, and I was the one who was going to have to tell his mother. I was the one who was going to have to stand next to her and console her at his funeral like he wasn't dead because of me.

"Aye boss, you probably shouldn't be here," one of my workers walked over to me and said, but I didn't give a fuck what that nigga was talking about because I needed answers, and I wasn't leaving until I got some.

I held a dismissive hand up to silence him, then I headed straight for the hazel eyed beauty. "Excuse me, do you have a second?" I asked her because I'd learned that you caught more flies with honey. I knew that if I spoke to her the way my partners in here were speaking to everyone, it was likely that she would call security and have us removed.

She glanced back at the other members of the medical staff then placed her small hand on my shoulder, then escorted me to the only area of the lobby that wasn't crowded. "What can I do for you?" she asked as she looked directly in my eyes waiting on me to answer her question.

Now, don't get me wrong, I was a nigga from the streets, but she had me feeling like a sucka just looking into her eyes. I'd never been lost in the stare of a bitch alone, yet here I was looking at this woman all gullible and shit. I needed to get myself together quick before she thought I was some lame nigga or something.

"I need to see what you can tell me about-"

"Let me stop you right there, sir." She held up her hand to silence me catching me completely off guard in the process. "I cannot give you any information about any patient, past, present, or future." She shook her head as she spoke.

Before I could respond to her, someone began to speak over the intercom. "Trauma team T2! Trauma team room T2!" The hazel eyed beauty's eyes widened as she heard the message over the intercom, then she gave me an apologetic look.

"I'm sorry, but I'm needed in the back. Please clear out of here. Only immediate family will be allowed back to see any patient here because of any type of violent crime," she said then walked away quickly leaving me stuck on stupid all over again as I watched her walk away.

I balled my fist up, and it involuntarily came up to my mouth, and I bit down on it. I'd given anything to slide up in that, and she looked like she could take all ten inches that I had to offer. "Aye, God!" I heard, but I was still staring in the direction that she'd just walked off in even though she was no longer in my view. "God!" I heard again, then turned my head in that direction.

"Aye man, where the hell you been?" I asked No Good as soon as I saw him. He had a real bad habit of disappearing when shit got tough, and I was ready to call him out on it.

"Man, some shit popped off down at my baby mama's crib, man. Nigga down there hitting on her and shit in front of my son, but look, what happened here?" No Good responded, and I just stared at him for several seconds before responding.

"Can't call it right now, my nigga," I responded as I looked past him just in time to see one of my young niggas by the name of Nuk slap the shit out of one of the nurses.

"Fuck!" I yelled as I ran over to him then threw him up against the wall. "The fuck is wrong with you, nigga?" I asked as I maintained a tight grip on his shirt. He attempted to break free at first, but he calmed down with a quickness once he realized who I was. "Get the fuck out of here, bruh before you get locked the fuck up!" I snapped, then let him go.

I kept my eyes trained on him as he ran out of the hospital. "Aye, everybody, clear out!" I yelled out so everybody that worked underneath me could leave the building. They were too damn rowdy in here, and we didn't need any more heat on us.

After they left mumbling under their breaths, I walked over to the woman who had been slapped. She had her hand over her face, but I took her hand into mine. "I'm truly sorry about that," I said as I looked down at her nametag and saw Tiffany printed out on it.

"It's fine," Tiffany said as she attempted to walk away, but I grabbed her arm softly.

"There was a nurse out here when I first got here. She has hazel eyes and is about this tall." I showed her with my hand how tall the woman was. "What's her name?" I asked, but she looked nervous. "I assure you, I just want to get to know her," I said then brushed her chin slightly with my thumb.

“Tameka,” she said, then looked back as if she was making sure that nobody heard her. “Tameka Taylor,” she continued, and I nodded my head with a slight smirk on my face.

“Take it easy, Tiffany,” I said as I backed away from her. Tameka Taylor had definitely piqued my interest, and I needed to get back to the house so I could figure out everything that I needed to know about her.

# JEWELZ

I was checking in on a couple of my patients when I heard, "Trauma team T2! Trauma team needed in T2!" I helped Mrs. Allison back to her bed and went to scrub up and put on my gloves so I could help. *Damn, this is like the third trauma we have had today. What is really going on?*

I put on my blue hair net and cap, slipped on my blue surgical jacket, and took two hair nets and slipped them over each one of my shoes, which was required attire when you were a trauma nurse or surgical nurse. I rushed down the hall to the trauma room, but the rest of the team was already rushing out the room wheeling the gurney. My coworker, Cindy was on top of the gurney on her knees giving chest compressions to the patient. "Follow us, Tameka to OR 1, we need you!" Cindy yelled out.

I turned on my heels following them to the OR room. If you've never been in an operating room before, let me tell you everybody has a job to do. We all grabbed the sheet and transferred him to the operating table. It was the first time I saw his face up close, and he didn't look to be any more than twenty-one, twenty-two. Marion cut his clothes off while I placed the oxygen mask on his face. "Come on, people. Let's save a life!" Dr. Briggs yelled, causing everyone to step up the process. He instructed Cindy to get a line started on him, but she was tired, and her hands were shaking from doing all those chest compressions. I pushed her out the way and took over. It didn't take me but about thirty seconds to hit the vein and start the antibiotics flowing through his system.

Whoever he was, he was a fighter. You could clearly see he had three shots to the center mass of his body. He was breathing on his own, but just barely. Dr. Briggs used the scalpel and tried to remove the bullets from his chest, but he started convulsing and never gained consciousness. I heard the machine flatlining, and my mind immediately went back to my husband lying on that cold slab in the morgue. I was filled with sadness and guilt. I was one of the best nurses in this hospital, and I wasn't there to save my own husband.

I ran around to the other side of the room and got the crash cart and turned the machine on, turning the button to five-hundred. "Clear!" I screamed, putting the paddles to his chest to give his heart a jumpstart. I watched his body rise and fall, and still nothing. I turned it up to seven-hundred. "Clear!" I screamed, hitting him again with the paddles, and still nothing. I didn't want him to die "Tameka, stop it right now, he is gone!" Dr. Briggs yelled at me. Cindy grabbed me from the back in a tight embrace while Marion grabbed the paddles from my hands. "It's okay, baby girl, he is gone. We did all we could," Cindy explained, walking me out the operating room.

Right outside the door, my emotions got the best of me as I slid down the wall pulling my hat off. I hated losing or feeling helpless, and that was exactly how I was feeling. "I know what was going through your head, it was too soon to come back, love," Cindy expressed with empathy. We talked for a minute till Tiffany passed by and told me Creep was out of surgery and asking for me.

I jumped to my feet. In the midst of everything going on, I was happy to know that he was well enough to ask for me and apparently say his name because I was sure Tiffany didn't know before then. "I'm sorry, Cindy. I have to go visit a friend, but thanks for the talk. We will catch up later," I said before walking to the nurses' desk to see what room he was in.

I walked to the computer and put in his real name, Antonio Macky. I made it my business to know everyone in the crew's real name, addresses, and birthdates, just for emergencies like this or if I had to bail them out of jail. I saw he was in Critical Care around the corner in Room 6.

I told my coworker I would be back, but I had my work phone on me. She nodded, and I went about my way. I walked around the desk and down the hallway till I reached Room 6. I slowly pushed the door, careful not to wake him if he was sleep, but to my surprise, he was wide awake. When he saw me, his eyes lit up, and he gave me a weak smile. I knew he was weak; he had lost a lot of blood.

I walked over to the bed and asked him how he was feeling, which was a stupid question.

"Happy to be alive," Creep confessed.

"I am too, bruh. I'm glad you okay with your crazy ass always on the front-line type nigga." We shared a laugh until he started coughing. I jumped up to get him some water, but by the time I poured it, the coughing had passed.

"Listen Jewelz, I was hoping I pulled through because I have something to tell you."

He had my full attention now. "What is it, Creep?" I asked curiously.

"Well, before the shooting started, I looked towards the street, you know me, I always pay attention to my surroundings," Creep said.

"Yes, I know. It's one if the main reasons I hired you to be at the house," I admitted.

He sat up a little bit like he was trying to get comfortable, but from the look on his face, it didn't seem to be working." Are you okay? Do you need more pain meds?" I asked him.

"Yes, I will be okay," he replied. "I was going to tell you that I got a good look at one of the guys in the car…"

"Yes? What did he look like? Do you know who it is?" I questioned.

"It w-aaas…" he never got to finish his sentence before his eyes widened and his body began shaking and jerking uncontrollably. "Oh shit, not again." I hit the intercom button on the side of his bed. "I need some help in here! Hurry up, he is coding!" I screamed. It didn't take long before doctors and nurses rushed the room. "Stay with me, Creep," I whispered in his ear trying to hold him down so they could get the medicine in his IV.

# NO GOOD

I walked out the house feeling like I was the shit. I was dressed from head to toe in Salvatore Ferragamo slacks with a button-down Jeffrey Rudes shirt. I had on my Berluti dress shoes to match my fit. I went and hopped in my 2017 Impala to hit the streets. It was a beautiful sunny day, clear blue skies. I pulled up to a red light and had to pull down the visor to block the sun from blinding my eyes. A car full of women pulled up next to me, one of them waved at me. I nodded my head towards them as the light turned green, and I pulled off. Hitting another red light, the same car pulled up, and one of the girls signaled for me to roll down my window. I let it down and said, "What's up, ma?"

The passenger smiled at me while saying, "That's what I'm trying to find out."

"And what exactly is it that you are trying to find out, sweetheart?" I asked her.

"The light finna turn green, so pull over so I can get out and holla at you," she said.

Once it turned green, I nodded and crossed over in front of their car. Finding a place where both cars could pull over, I put my hazards on and pulled over. I put my car in park and waited for her to come to the car. I grabbed my gun because these days, no one could be trusted. Not knowing what her real motive could have been, I wasn't going to be caught slipping. As she walked towards me, she looked sexy as fuck. She had the look of Nia Long but thicker, more ass and bigger tits. Her walk was sexy as fuck; it made you wonder how good she could ride a dick.

Approaching my window, she leaned down on the side of the door and saw the gun on my door saying, "Damn, it's like that?'

"No ma, it ain't like that, but I don't go nowhere without my strap."

"I guess I can understand with all the killing that's been going on here lately."

"Are you from around here, ma?"

"I was born and raised here, but I bounced back and forth between here and Texas most of my older life."

"Oh, that's what's up, I got some people out in Dallas and Houston."

"That's where I lived almost half my life was in Dallas."

"What's your people's last name?"

"Johnson and Jones."

"That's what up, mine is the Jackson family."

"Damn, the Jackson family real big out there. You kin to James Jackson?"

"Yea, that's my uncle."

The driver of the car she was in honked the horn, and she looked toward her and yelled, "Bitch, hold on," in a playful way, then looked back to me.

"Lock my number in your phone."

I grabbed my phone from the center console and unlocked it. I looked at her and asked her what her name was.

"My name is Brandy, but everyone calls me Pretty."

I locked her number in and then laughed.

"What you laughin' for?"

"I'm laughing because the name does fit you. You is pretty as a mutherfucka."

"What's your name?"

"They call me No Good."

"Hmmm… do that name fit you?"

"Stick around, ma, and you can find out."

"Aight, but let me go before these hoes start trippin'.""

"Aight, I will hit you later."

She walked off and got in the car. I pulled off while bumping some Boosie in my system.

I hit a couple corners and pulled up to one of the spots. I parked and jumped out. I walked in the spot, and niggas was talking about Jap. I kind of felt bad because Jap was a young nigga, but now wasn't the time for a pity party because I was ready to get down to business. I said what's up to all the niggas and then looked at the lieutenant and told him I was there to pick up. He got up and went to the back room and walked back out with MGM bookbag filled with the money.

I dumped the bag of money on the table and told the niggas to count up. The lieutenant was used to just handing the bag over to God, and he would just leave out with it, but this wasn't God's call any more, this was my show, and it was a new order. I was going to make sure before I left out of each spot that everything was accounted for.

The lieutenant looked at the homies and told them, "You heard what the nigga said, what the fuck y'all waiting for? Count that shit up."

I could tell they wanted to say something, but they weren't going to say something to him. It wasn't their job to question orders given from higher up, but we all could see that the lieutenant wasn't happy about having the money counted up either. I stood right over them niggas watching them count every single dollar. Once all fifty-thousand was accounted for, I had them put it back in the bag. I grabbed it and left out the spot.

I got back into my car, hit a few more corners, and stopped at the stash spot to put the fifty-thousand up. After I put the money up, I left and headed and went to grab something to eat. I went to the drive thru at Chic fil a. I ordered me a number four, and when I pulled up to pay, I licked my lips, and the girl at the window almost dropped my damn food she was staring so damn hard. I snatched my food, put the bag on the passenger seat, and told her to be more careful next time, looking so damn hard almost made my food fall. She turned red from embarrassment, so I blew her a kiss and pulled off laughing. I loved to fuck with thirsty bitches.

I had a few more spots to go pick up some money at, so I was going to eat on the go.

I got out the car and went up in the last spot to get the money. They had a house full of hoes dancing like it was a mutherfuckin' strip club. I shut the music off and yelled, "Get your fuckin' clothes and get the fuck out of here!" They ran up out that bitch fast as shit.

"You niggas betta not be up in here trickin' off my mutherfuckin' money on these bitches. I know one thing; the count better be right. Go get that shit," I said to the lieutenant.

He walked back to the room I was in with the bag, and I still wasn't done talking shit. I had to add so he got the point of what was not going to happen up in this shit.

"You dumb ass niggas got the music blasting didn't even hear me walk in the fuckin' house. I could have been twelve or the ops running up in here to take everything, and you so busy looking at dirty ass you wouldn't have known till it was too late. If you want to go chase ass, then leave now. I am sure I know a hundred niggas that would love to jump in your shoes."

They had counted it without me having to tell them. They already knew I was mad. It had forty grand in it.

"How you only got forty thousand in here when this spot more lit than the one on the east side/. Let me find one of you are fucking around with the money, it's going to be some problems. They just handed me 50 stacks and ain't out of product yet, y'all talkin' about needing more soon. What is going on in here?"

One of the youngtas said, "If you goin' make me go through all this, I can go fuck with—"

I looked at him, and he didn't finish.

"That's right, lil' nigga. Watch your fuckin mouth."

If only he knew what was going through my mind. I wanted to go in my waist and pull out my gun and shoot him in his face, but I knew I had a temper I needed to ease up with, so before I acted on my thoughts, I grabbed the bag and left out of there.

I hopped in my car and called my road dog. The phone just rung, rung, rung, and then went to the voicemail. By the time I went to hit the end button to call him back, he was trying to call me. I was so mutherfuckin' hot. Instead of me with the usual what's up my nigga, I answered like,

"You know this lil' nigga got the nerve to tell me," before I could finish, God cut me off and told me to meet him at the lounge. Agreeing, I said okay, and I headed that way.

# GOD

I knew my nigga, so I knew something was wrong, but whatever it was, from the tone in his voice, it wasn't something to be talked about over the phone. I wasn't finna think too hard to figure out what was going on, I was just going to wait until he got here. I was sitting at my table watching Cheryl watch me. While she was thinking about me, I was thinking about Tameka. At the same time, I wouldn't mind fucking Cheryl tonight; she did have some good ass pussy and some of the best sloppy toppy head. She just came with too much drama. The more she watched me, the more I thought about going to her house and fucking the shit out of her when it was time to lock up. Actually, I was ready to get deep in her guts now, so I called her over to the table. I told her to have someone cover the bar real quick and meet me in the storage room. She already knew what was 'bout to happen; it wasn't the first time I dragged her ass back there. I got up and walked back and had my pants to my knees when she walked in.

Knowing the drill, she squatted and began to do her magic. Slobbering while sucking and licking. I knew I didn't have time for a long session, and the way she was working her jaws was making me want to nut already. I pulled out her mouth and slid on a condom. I turned her around. She grabbed onto the metal pole of the shelving unit I had installed for the cases of our high-end bottles of liquor. She put one leg up on two cases of Corona that was next to her and bent over. She had nothing on under that short ass skirt, but fuck it, easier access. I took my finger and slid it across her slit to make sure she was wet enough for me to just slide in, and as always, she was ready. I placed both my hands on her hips and slammed into her pussy rough and aggressively causing her to yell out. I was giving her long, deep, hard strokes, and had I not had a grip on her waist as tight as I did, she would have either slipped and busted her ass, or went head first into the bottles on the shelf.

She tried to throw her ass back, but I was fucking her so good and hard, she couldn't handle it. I used my hands that were on her waist and moved them so I could spread her ass cheeks so I could see my dick slide in and out. I knew it was feeling good to her because my shit was coated already with her wetness. After another ten minutes, I came and pulled out. I tied the condom in a knot and wrapped it up in a napkin from a pack of them we had in the back. I walked to the employee bathroom and flushed it and washed my hands and fixed my pants.

When I walked out from the back, No Good was already sitting at my table just shaking his head because I was sure like the few other people that were inside, there was no doubt they heard Cheryl's cries from me beating the pussy up. A few minutes later, Cheryl came out limping doing the walk of shame and went back to work, but this time, she wasn't staring at me because she was embarrassed.

When I sat down, No Good spoke to me,

"So, you hit it again, I see."

"She kept eye fucking me, so I said fuck it and gave her what she wanted while I was waiting for you."

"Now that bitch goin' be stalking and following you around again," he said laughing.

"Nah, because I'm going to have a long talk with her tomorrow. You know I don't got time for the bullshit."

"If you ain't got time for the bullshit, you wouldn't have stuck yo' nasty ass dick up in her again."

"Nasty ass dick? Nigga, who you talkin' to? Do you wanna compare? At least my hoes got class, you fuck gutta hoes. Alleyway rats."

"Yeah, but all my bitches are bad though."

"You right, bad for your health."

"Enough with the clowning, let me tell you about this lil' nigga Ron Ron, goin' tell me if I'm going to push him around the way I do, he goin' go fuck around with somebody else."

"So, the nigga said them exact words?"

"Well, not those exact one's. I gave him a look which made him stop mid-sentence."

"You already know that nigga got to go."

"Yeah, I know, I was going to do it right then in front of everybody, but I aint got time to be taking out a whole house."

"We need to get on top of that ASAP before that nigga link up with someone and tell them our business."

No Good got up, gave me dap, and left out. I got up getting ready to leave my damn self, and I got a text from one of my lieutenants telling me he needed to talk to me as soon as possible. I walked towards the exit door, and Cheryl looked at me, and I smiled at her. She put her head down. The homie only got at me when it was something important, so I knew I needed to go check him.

I got in my car and headed to the spot. I went in, and he began to tell me about how No Good dumped the money on the table making them count the money up and was demanding shit all ignorant. He wanted to just deal with me because he could tell that No Good was going to be difficult to work with. I told the homie that I was going to talk to No Good, and if he kept on trippin' out then, I would see to it that I did the pickups for this spot only.

"Good looking out, God," the lieutenant said.

# MONTANA

I had been sitting in the parking lot of the hospital for some time. I heard from one of my homies in the crew that my nigga Creep had gotten shot at Jewelz's house. I wanted to go inside and see if he was alright, but I knew Jewelz was back at work, and I had a feeling that her and LA were becoming suspicious of my involvement with Montez's death.

It felt like my team was turning on me when I needed them the most. I had thoughts of starting my own crew, but almost every nigga that I would want on my team was already linked with somebody else. Sure, I could get me some shooters easily with all these young, hungry ass niggas out here with little or no money, but that wasn't what I was looking for. I needed people that were ruthless, heartless. I needed people that didn't have no reservation about laying down no one, men, women, children, old folks. No one was exempt from the plans I had in my mind.

I was just about to light my blunt up when my eyes zoomed in on someone coming out the hospital and coming towards me. "I know him," I mumbled to myself. I knew who he was from niggas I worked around and watching him and his boys turn up in the club, I also knew he worked for God's crew.

Because a little while back Montez thought that one of our workers, C Note was being shady and trying to play both sides because he had been seen several times in the neighborhood and our people knew that area was off limits to them, so we watched and followed him for about a month, plus we paid a couple of smokers for information on the crew and to find out if C Note was dealing over there. It turned out to be nothing, but his baby mama lived in the neighborhood.

But we did hear a lot about this dude, Legend who was now walking past my car engrossed in a heated conversation and pulling on a cigarette like it was giving him new life. I watched him carefully in my rearview mirror go stand in front of the smoking pit. It was an enclosed area shaped like a bus stop where people could smoke away from the hospital. If I was going to approach him, I needed to do it when he was alone, but you couldn't just walk up to a street nigga and start a conversation.

I got out my car and headed over to where he was pacing back and forth talking on the phone. I went inside the pit and sat on the bench. I reached inside my jacket and pulled out my Al Capone cigars. "Aye, bruh! You got a light I can use right quick?" I asked him. He looked at me with a strong mug on his face. "Nigga, first off, I'm not your damn bruh. Second, don't you see me on the phone with your rude ass?" Legend spat, angrily tossing the lighter at me.

I caught it in midair. Yeah, this nigga had a serious attitude. I lit my cigar and puffed it, listening in on the conversation he was carrying on. Within minutes, I gathered that there were some problems going on with God's organization and that Legend was very unhappy about the way things were being ran. To me, that was music to my ears, but that still didn't mean that he would turn on them for me. I played my position and sat quietly puffing my cigar until he hung up the phone. "Aye, young blood, you know, I can help you with your situation."

He bomb rushed me pushing me up against the wall with his forearm against my throat. "Why the fuck you in my business? Are you a cop or something?" Legend asked checking my pockets with his free hand. "Hold up, let me explain, it's nothing like that. I just feel like we can help each other out," I said calmly, and he loosened his grip.

"Look, I know who you are and what you are about which is the only reason I didn't kill you for putting your hands on me and being disrespectful," I said straightening my shirt back up. "My name is Montana Cortez. I'm the co-founder of the Taylor Made boy's." I reached my hand out as a friendly gesture, but he didn't accept. Instead, he stood there staring me down like I was beneath him.

"Touché, my nigga, touché. I understand, never fraternize with the competition," I retorted. "It's not a good look for us to be seen together, so meet me at Club Sanabella tonight on Simpson Road at eight if you want to change your situation."

***

I had been at the bar inside the Sanabella drinking shots of Vodka since about 7:30, I had to get my head back in the game and figure out what I was going to do about getting these Russians and now Italians their money.

My girl called me today shortly after I left the hospital and said someone had broken in and trashed her house, but they didn't take anything, they just slashed all the couches and comforters, pillows, broke mirrors and pictures, but the one thing that stood out the most was they took our family portrait that was hanging on the wall and carved X's through all of all faces. There was no way I could leave Erica and my daughter in harm's way, so I took them to my sister's house where I knew they would be safe, even though me and my sister didn't really get along anymore, I knew if I had problems, her and her husband, Drama would not let anything happen to Erica and Nik-Nik.

Looking down at my watch, it was 8:39, and I hadn't seen this nigga Legend yet. I ordered me another shot from Stephanie the bartender and went to the bathroom. I stumbled a little getting off the stool, but I could hold my liquor, so I knew I was alright. I headed to the bathroom to take a piss and take a one on one with my nose. The cocaine would definitely give me a pick me up.

There was a couple of dudes in there, so I went to the stall, sat down, and I pulled out my cigarette case dumping some of the cocaine on it using my credit card to make even lines. I rolled up a dollar bill and inhaled deeply clearing the line completely. I repeated the process on the other side. "Whew!" I yelled from the burn and the rush it gave me immediately. I sat there stuck and in a daze for a few minutes before I could move.

I walked out the stall to the sink to wash my hands and dry them. I walked out the bathroom feeling like a new man with a smile on my face. Before I made it back to my seat at the bar, I saw Legend standing there with a fine ass young lady ordering drinks. He was looking around and spotted me, throwing his head up in a nod as I approached them. I nodded back. "Glad you could make it, my nigga, and who is this lovely lady you have with you?" I questioned because I didn't want to talk business in front of everybody. "Oh, this wifey right here, no need to concern yourself with her--she is here to have a good time," Legend responded.

"There is a booth right there in the corner we can sit over there and discuss some business," I retorted leading the way.

"Sabrine, you can go dance while we talk shop, baby," Legend told her giving her a kiss on the lips and she went about her way while we took a seat at the booth.

"So, Mr. Cortez what is that you think you can help me with, and why did you choose me to come at?" Legend asked before I could say a word.

I sat quietly sipping on my drink and thought about how to say what was on my mind. "Let's just say I'm having some financial problems, and my team is not on my side, so since they don't have my back, I'm trying to put together a team to take it all" I spoke seriously. Legend burst into laughter. "Nigga, I have done my research on you too, and from what I know, since your boss man was killed, his little brother LA and his wife is running shit with an iron fist. It will be damn near impossible for you to take them down," Legend responded, still laughing at my plan.

"You let me worry about them, I can pay you very well if you can get me a loyal team together. I need some heavy hitters that won't run or turn at the first sign of trouble, can you do it?" I asked Legend. "How much money are you talking, because if it ain't worth my time, I can get up and leave now?" he asked.

"A million," I replied looking him in the eyes.

"A million, huh?" he repeated. "I wonder how you can pay me a million, but you can't pay these niggas with a price on your head," Legend asked nodding his head and playing with the napkin up under his drink.

"Easy, I'm going to rob all the main trap spots if you can get me the people I need, that way I can pay you and my debts off," I confessed.

"How about you give me your number, and I will see what I can do, but to be honest, I don't know too many niggas in the city that will go up against the Taylor Made boys that's not already affiliated with another crew," Legend admitted.

"Don't look for niggas in the city then. I know you know people all over--that's why I came to you," I told him.

We sat there chopping it up about our plans on how to get money for more than two hours, then we made plans to meet up again in a couple days to see where we stood. "I only have a week to get to this money up, so I need you to move quickly," I informed Legend before I got up to leave, but not before I gave him my number to keep in touch. I was confident that he would come through for me.

# JEWELZ

After everything that happened at the hospital yesterday, my emotions were all over the place. Cindy made me leave for the rest of day after Creep coded on me right after one of our patients died. She felt like the stress was too much.

I was never one to feel helpless and needy, but yesterday had me feeling some type of way. I never felt so alone and unloved in my life. I knew LA was there for me no matter what, but it wasn't the same as being with my husband or my family. I came home, spoke to the guys that were protecting me and my house, I explained to them what had happened with Creep, then went and took a long, hot shower. I threw on some leggings and a t-shirt and laid across the bed.

I couldn't focus on anything but the negative, so I got up and got my cellphone out my Fendi purse and called Gabrielle and Pamela on the three way to tell them about my day, of course they already knew about the shooting at the house because they had come over after I left, but I know they wanted an update on what was going on with Creep.

I called Gabrielle first, then Pamela. "Hey boo, how are you holding up?" Pamela asked first, then Gabrielle right behind her. "Y'all, today has been crazy. I lost a patient, then Creep was doing well, talking and everything. He was just about to describe the person he saw before the shooting started, and he started coding on me."

"What?" Gabrielle shouted.

"Is he alright, or he didn't make it?" Pamela asked. I got silent before I answered because I didn't have a current update myself. "Cindy sent me home, but he was in surgery when I left," I explained.

"It's something wrong with her, Gabrielle," Pamela said. "I know. You want us to come over, Jewelz?" Gabrielle asked.

"Yeah," I said a little more cheerful. See, this was why I loved these girls. They knew me better than myself sometimes. I didn't have to tell them what I was feeling because they could sense it. About an hour later, I heard them in the living room harassing the guys like they were known to do, so I got up and went in the front to grab us a bottle of Ciroc and some juice for our session.

We sat and talked for hours. I told them about my husband's letter and how he stated that I needed to watch my back from everyone, and how he was starting to think that Montana had bad intentions towards him, and the fact that nobody knew who this dude God was, but I thought he was the key to finding out what really happened that night.

They agreed that my concerns were valid and that I needed to switch up the operation again because if Montana was moving foul, he knew everything about the setup and the shipments. It would be easy for him to try and intercept them and take over. We all went in the living room to have a talk with everybody that was there, and LA and Lawless started moving things around immediately.

LA said he had tried to reach out to Montana several times and got no response, so it led him to believe that something was going on with him too. Lawless said a couple weeks ago Montana had come by the trap house and tried to collect the money a day early, but LA had changed up and already picked it up the cash and transferred the drugs. "This wis so unlike Montana not to come around us, especially me, after his best friend died," I told the room.

"Jewelz, don't take this the wrong way, but you are not stupid, you are just blinded by your grief. Montana has been acting shady since the beginning; he didn't even shed a tear at the funeral," Gabrielle stated.

"Even though nobody else will be bold enough to say it, we have all been thinking it. Montana had something or everything to do with Montez's death, and if you sit down and think about it, you will see it too," Pamela said out loud.

There was a lot of head nods, and you rights being said. I went to bed last night thinking about all that had been said and revealed, and I felt like shit. I had fucked the nigga that killed my husband, and on the same night he did it. I know Montez must be turning over in his grave, but today was a new day, and I was going to get Mr. Montana Cortez if it was the last thing I did.

I got up to shower and get ready for work. I was going in early so I could go check on Creep. I got dressed and went in the kitchen to make me some lunch. I didn't have to, but I hated the food at the hospital. I fixed me some chicken and broccoli alfredo with some Hawaiian rolls and corn in three separate containers. I grabbed my lunch bag, put the containers inside, picked up my keys, and headed out the door. LA had the crew already outside on guard, and he was standing by my car dressed in all Rocawear.

"Good morning, sis. You ready to go?" he greeted. I wasn't aware he had plans on going with me, but I knew trying to object would be pointless, so I tossed him my keys and went to the passenger side to get in. The drive to the hospital was quiet except for the radio playing. I could tell we both had things on our mind. I was worried about Creep. I prayed that he pulled through because he was the only one that could identify the person that tried to kill me.

LA pulled up to the hospital thirty minutes later and let me out in front by the entrance." I will be in after I park the car, sis," LA said. I nodded my head in acknowledgement. I walked in the door and to the break room to put my lunch in the fridge and bumped into Marion, my coworker. "Hey Tameka, how are you feeling today?"

"I'm good, Marion. Thanks for asking," I replied, trying to cut the small talk and make it out the door."

"Okay, see you around," he said before I bolted out the break room.

I walked over to the desk where Tiffany was sitting updating charts in the computer. I really didn't care for her messy ass, but I tried to remain professional at all times.

"Hey chic, how is it going today?" I spoke while keying in Creep's government name. He was on the second floor in critical care, thank God he was okay. I read down a little farther to see what was documented. According to the records, he had to have a blood transfusion but was awake and able to speak. "Yes!" I yelled and did a little dance I was so happy. *I don't know if I could take losing someone else close to me*, I thought taking the elevator upstairs.

I got off at the second floor and went to his room. When I opened the door, he was sound asleep. I walked over slowly trying not to wake him up. I knew his body had been through a lot, and he was probably heavily medicated. I lifted the chair that was next to his bed and turned it around so I could watch him. I pulled out my phone to text LA the room number. "Jewelz, you came back," I heard in a weak voice. I looked up from the phone and smiled. "You knew I was, we never leave our family alone," I said just as LA walked in the door.

"Damn right, we Taylor Made," LA repeated walking to the other side of the bed to get a closer look at the damage the hospital had done to Creep. Montez and LA hated hospital and thought that doctors let poor people die because they couldn't pay. If that was true, I made sure that nobody in our crew had to worry about that. I paid whatever medical expenses they had in cash money.

"I'm glad you came with her LA because I don't know who this person is, but I got a good look at them because I heard them say, "Oh that is that bitch right there," Creep explained.

"So, what did he look like?" I asked curiously. "He is brown-skinned with Burgundy locs, and some strange green eyes with a tattoo on his face." When Creep said that, if felt like all the breath in my body had left. Burgundy locs and dark green eyes? That was no other than Money.

"How did he find me after all these years, and what could he possibly want with me now?"

Jewelz, are you okay?" LA yelled, breaking me out my daze. I grabbed my cellphone and ran out the room. I had to call my goon bitches, Gabrielle, Pamela, and our secret one we only communicated with her over the phone, but when it was serious business, she always sent help.

After I told them I had a problem and what it was, LA stepped out in the hallway. "Jewelz, don't worry about nothing, me and the boys will find out who this nigga is and deal with it the same way my brother would, if not worse," LA barked. I couldn't let LA get involved in this. He had no idea how ruthless Money Mitchell could be. He would kill them all just for being associated with me. His only weakness was pussy, so I knew I had to handle this.

# MONEY

**Money:** "Aye dog, thanks for the information. Pretty soon, Jewelz Santana and her little punk ass crew won't be a problem for you no more. Come by the spot, I got a little bounty money for you later on."

**Montana:** "No problem, see you soon. but be careful. Don't get caught slippin', she is more than she appears to be. A lot has changed; she is a goon bitch."

I was laying on my bed, I had my shirt lifted up past my stomach, my sweat pants pulled down to my knees. Pam had her head in between my legs trying to do her best sucking my dick. I had my hand on her head pushing it further down, she was trying to pull her head back because she couldn't handle the length I had. She was focused on just the head for the past fifteen minutes. I was close to just making her get up and go home. I was bored. It was times like this that I would think back to Jewelz. She gave me the best head I ever had, no one could suck my dick like she could. Just thinking about that deceitful bitch was making my dick go soft. That was the reason I was trying to force Pam's head down so I could at least get a nut off. My time was valuable, and I wasted enough of it with her just playing, so I was going to help her mouth get me off.

Finally, she was getting used to my size, and it began to feel good. I was about to cum when I heard my phone going off. I wasn't going to make Pam stop because like I said, she was actually in a zone, and I was about to bust. My phone wasn't letting up, so I looked at it to see who it was blowing me up. Depending on how important the caller was would determine if I answered or not. Seeing a name pop up across the screen had me wondering what Montana could want. I hadn't heard from him in a long time since his childhood friend had got released from jail. The nerve this nigga had calling me. When Jewelz took off and disappeared on me was the same night his boy had an appointment with her. After that, none of them was heard from or seen again.

I answered to see what this muthafucka wanted. He must be really crazy to be calling me. Even though I had no proof he played a part in her getting away from me, I didn't need any.

"Speak," I said into the phone with Pam still sucking my dick. She looked up at me giving me a look like *really?* She was a new bitch I brought onto the roaster, but if she knew better, she wouldn't question me, or I'd knock her head off.

"Money, I need to holla at you. You busy?" Montana asked me.

"Actually, I am. I have my dick in my bitch's mouth, so hurry the fuck up and tell me what the fuck you callin' me for. It better be good too."

"It's about Jewelz. You still looking for her? I may be able to help you."

When he said that, he had my full attention. I pushed Pam away and pulled my pants up. She just sucked her teeth, walked her ass out my room, and closed the door.

"You have my attention, it better be worth it because you just fucked up my nut."

"Oh, it's worth it. How much are you willing to pay for her whereabouts?" Montana said.

"So, you tax me after everything I done for you?" I responded.

"No, I'm not trying to tax you, I know you eat well off these bitches. I'm just looking for a little something off the top for leading you to your top money maker."

"I'll throw you $500," I told him.

Montana laughed saying, "You're joking, right? You meant more like five bands?"

"I'm dead serious. What makes you think I want that bitch that bad that I would give up $5000 for her whereabouts?'

"The way she was acting when I bumped into her and asked about you let me know you want her for something," he said back trying to make it look like he didn't know where she'd been, but I would play along with him.

I may be a pimp, but I'm also a gangsta, and I knew how these kind of niggas rolled. If I didn't pay what he was asking, then he wouldn't give up no information. Sitting thinking it over, trying to decide if she was worth the money, I was getting madder and madder. All the money I lost when she took off, plus I hadn't had my dick sucked as good as she could just made my mind up, and I knew I was going to pay Montana the money he was asking. I couldn't wait to get my hands on that bitch.

"Tell me where you at. I'm on my way right now," I said

Montana replied, "In Cali."

"Cali, what the fuck you mean, Cali? I didn't know I was gonna have to leave the state, but I want that bitch, so I'll be out there in a few hours." Here I was thinking I had to just get in my car and drive to him. Now, it looked like I had to book a flight.

"Okay, hit me back on this number when you land, Money." I just hung up. I rubbed my hands together thinking how good it would feel to see the fear in her eyes. I yelled for Pam to come back into my room. She came rushing in, but once I told her to pack me a bag, she frowned. I knew she was hoping I was going to fuck her little ass, but that was the last thing on my mind.

***

I walked out the airport. I got in a taxi so they could bring me to the rental place for me to pick up a car. I was anxious to meet up with Montana and go get this bitch, but this was a new state, and I didn't know her circumstances. I couldn't just run up on her the way I really wanted to. Getting out the taxi, I walked into Enterprise and stood in line. I was glad I made a reservation, but it looked like a lot of people in here were mad they couldn't get what they wanted. Going to the next person available, I gave them my reservation number, and patiently waited to be told to wait outside for them to pull up my car. Once I got outside, I was pleased with my choice in car. I was here not to draw attention to myself, so I got a basic economy vehicle. I put my luggage in the trunk and walked to get in the car. I drove off following the GPS to the five-star hotel I was staying in. I could get away with a basic car, but I couldn't stay in no run-down hotel.

I laid on the bed to catch a few hours of sleep. I got up three hours later and called Montana. He answered the phone on the third ring.

"What's up, my nigga, you made it out here?"

"Yeah, I'm out here. What time can we meet up?"

"Whatever time you ready to pay me. I'm going to take you straight to her job," he told me.

"I'm ready to pay you now, but I'm not giving you shit until I lay eyes on Jewelz," I told him.

"So, where you want to meet at?"

"We can meet at the Holiday Inn right down the street from the airport."

"Aight, I know where that's at. Give me about thirty minutes."

'I'll be right here waiting for you."

I hung my phone up and put it in my pocket. I was born at night, but not last night. I wasn't going to tell him where I was staying at. The Holiday Inn was fifteen minutes from where I was. I was going to leave from my room in like ten minutes, so we should arrive around the same time. Being a pimp, I was familiar with all hotels in every state that human trafficking was big in, and Cali was one of them. I had called my boy before I hit up Montana. I had left something out here the last time I was out here. I told him I needed him to meet me with that. I made it downstairs and to my car. Pimpin' Jay was running late. I was about to pull off in two minutes, but just as I was starting the car up, he pulled up. He got in the passenger seat of the car I was driving and was trying to converse. I had to tell him we could catch up later, but I had some business to handle. He handed me my gun and got out my car, returning to his. He pulled off and beeped his horn, and I took off in the other direction.

I pulled into the Holiday Inn and parked. Maybe two minutes later, Montana was calling my phone, and I looked up. Before answering the phone, I wanted to peep his movements. I noticed a 745 pull in, but I knew that wasn't him, so I kept looking, and he called me again. This time, the driver of the car got out with a phone in his hand, and when I saw it was Montana, I was surprised. What the fuck he got going on out here that enabled him to push a car like that but needed $5000 from me?

I beeped the horn so he knew what car I was in. He walked to the passenger side and got in. He put his hand out to give me dap, but I didn't return the gesture.

"I didn't come all this way to bullshit with you, Montana. Where Jewelz at?"

"She's at work, let's go. She works at the hospital."

I backed the car out from where I was parked and jumped on the 105 freeway. I followed the directions Montana was giving, and finally, we pulled up into the hospital parking lot. We got out and walked inside, and he had me follow him down a few hallways, and somehow, we managed to be outside in sight of a nurses station, yet still in a little cut. We waited for about twenty minutes, and before I saw her, I heard her laugh. She was only thirty feet from me, and as bad as I wanted to choke the shit out of her right here and now, I knew it was best if I got out of here. I knew I couldn't do anything here at her job, but you could bet your life I was going to follow her from here. I tapped Montana and walked off the way we came in with him following behind me.

"I can't believe she is working. I had her name being ran for a while, and nothing came back."

"She changed her name legally," Montana informed me as we got back into my rental. I headed back to the Holiday Inn. When we got there, I handed him the envelope with the $5000 in all hundreds. His eyes grew, which didn't make sense to me because again, he was pushing a 745. Not really caring to ask, I was happy when he got out the car. He walked to his with a huge smile on his face and got in his car and took off. I looked at the time and noticed it was twelve. Knowing how hospital shifts normally worked, I wanted to get back to her job so I could follow her home. It would be safer to get here there.

I watched Jewelz walk out the front door of the hospital with a few other nurses. She was smiling and laughing. I thought to myself, *You wouldn't be smiling if you knew I was this close to your ass, now would you?* She got into a Range Rover, and I began to follow behind her. I had my hat down low in case she became suspicious and looked out her rearview mirror. When I saw her pull into the driveway to the huge house and get out, I knew she had a man who was running things. I was about to roll down the window and shoot her ass when I saw a few niggas come from nowhere and greet her, walking her in the house.

The next night, I thought maybe luck would be by myside, and I'd be able to catch her leaving for work. When I saw the same group of niggas outside her house, it pissed me off. They were fucking with my plans, so I opened fire on their asses. I knew one of them saw me. We locked eyes, but I wasn't worried. No one knew me, and I was sure he was hit and would be in a morgue in a few hours.

I decided to lay back for a few days. I lucked out when I went back by her house and saw Jewelz leaving, this time not in her work uniform, but she was dressed casually. I put the rental in drive and was ready to follow her. She drove to a little lounge, and I waited a few minutes before I got out the car and went inside. I ducked off into a dark corner and sat down watching her. I had my hat pulled down low. I was ready to snatch this bitch. At first, I just wanted to kill her, but now, I wanted to beat her ass, making her death long and painful. I knew I couldn't just make her come back with me, she would just run again. After a few drinks, she finally signaled to pay her bill and stood up to leave. Once she walked out the door, I followed behind her. She was walking toward her car, and I reached my hand out to grab her but was grabbed myself.

# GOD

I had some shit on my mind, I went to my table at the lounge watching the crowd. I was deep in thought over the events that had taken place recently. Tonight was a slow night, so watching what was going on was easy. I looked up at the door and saw Tameka walk in. She appeared to have a lot on her mind too. She headed directly to the bar and signaled for Cheryl to get her usual as she sat down. Right after she was sitting, I noticed a new face walk in, but it was clear he didn't want to be seen. That was the plus side to owning a place that wasn't big like other places, you were able to get familiar with faces and could tell when someone came in not wanting to be seen. He looked around and found a place where he could go undetected, but yet see everything around him. I picked up on this because that was exactly how I moved around. His behavior made it clear he was watching Tameka, so I was going to be keeping my eye on him.

I pulled my phone out and called No Good, and he answered right away.

"What's up, my nigga?" he said picking up.

"How far is you from the lounge?" I asked him.

"Shit, actually, I'm right around the corner. I was headed to you and figured I would find you there."

"I need you to post up in the parking lot and keep an eye on things outside just in case I need you."

'Say no more, my nigga."

I sat my phone back on the table. I put my shades on and leaned back like I was basically staring into space. But I actually had my eyes going back and forth from Tameka and the man watching her. Three minutes went by when No Good called me back to let me know he was parked outside.

I called Cheryl over to my table so I could order something to drink. I wanted to make myself look like I was a regular customer like everyone else. Cheryl came over with a smile on her face. Licking her lips, she asked me, "Hey, boss man, what can I get for you?"

"First, I need for you to act like I'm a regular customer, so drop the boss man for me, okay? Second, I need for you to bring me my usual, but I need for you to charge me."

"Ok, if you insist, but will you be tipping me?" she said laughing.

What she didn't know was nothing was funny about what I was doing right now. This wasn't no role play for her freaky ass. I was being serious. She walked off only to return four minutes later with my drink and picking up the $50 bill I had put on the table.

"Keep the change."

"If you keep tipping like this…you should do this more often."

"Cheryl, I really need you to take what I asked you seriously, okay? Act like I'm just a regular customer that you don't know."

As she was walking back towards the bar because a few people were looking for refills, I noticed the man still didn't order himself anything to drink. That was where he was messing up at--most places didn't allow someone to just sit and not get at least one drink. I noticed Tameka had ordered another drink, but this time, she got a shot as well. Thinking maybe this could be my opportunity to speak with her again, I took my drink down in one sip and held up the glass to let Cheryl know I needed a refill.

She walked to the table to bring it to me, and I told her to go see if that customer wanted something to drink. This time, I didn't pay for the drink. Hell, I had basically paid for it already. She went back to the bar first to make a drink and get a beer for a couple sitting a few seats down from Tameka. Cheryl rounded the bar and made her way to him. I could tell he declined a drink and just nodded his head. She smiled and went back. I picked up my phone and sent her a text thanking her.

No Good called me. Picking up the phone, I answered, "What's up?"

"How long you gonna have me sitting out here? Shit, I need a damn drink."

"Not much longer; it looks like it's almost time to move." I noticed that Tameka handed over her credit card to Cheryl indicating she was about to leave.

The man in the corner also took notice, and his body demeanor changed. Tameka laughed at whatever Cheryl said to her as she handed her back the card. Tameka got off the bar stool and made her way outside. As soon as she was out the door, just as I thought, the man got up walking out at a fast pace behind her. Cheryl had taken notice as well and looked right at me. I gave her the look that I was on it. I got up and left out as well.

I noticed No Good sitting up in his car already aware that something was about to go down.

Tameka must have felt someone following behind her because she turned around real fast and as soon as she did, and noticed who was behind her,

her eyes grew. She tried to reach for something in her purse, but she moved too slow, and the man had grabbed her. I was now where they were, and I spoke up.

"Aye ma, is you good?"

She looked at me and the look of terror in her eyes let me know this was someone she had dealt with before and was afraid of.

The man who now had her pinned against her car said. "This has nothing to do with you, so go back inside and mind your fucking business."

"You right, it's none of my business, but I'm not going to sit around and let a man put his hands on a woman."

"Well then, we gonna have a problem.'

I laughed, "You don't want these problems."

The nigga reached for a gun like anyone from the streets would do. What he didn't know was as we were going back and forth, No Good snuck up behind him and placed the barrel of his gun to the man's head.

"I wouldn't do that if I was you," No Good said.

The man threw his hands up, causing him to release Tameka. Tameka cocked her hand back and slapped the fuck out of him. He flinched like he wanted to do something, so No Good put him in a choke hold using his other arm.

I laughed again while reaching in his waist line. "I told you that you didn't want these problems. You have two options. You can try to make a move and die right here, or you can get in your car and get the fuck up out of here."

"All you have to do is let me go, and I'm gone," he said.

# JEWELZ

I was glad the two men intervened, giving me a chance to get away. I knew I had seen one of them before, but I couldn't remember where right now. I was shook as I sped to my house dialing every number I knew.

"What the fuck was Money doing in California? And how in the fuck did he know where to find me?" I asked myself.

I had been extremely careful after Creep gave me a description of him at the hospital, but I figured it was just a coincidence or that it was medicine he was on, or at least that's what I told myself. "Shit! I yelled hitting the steering wheel. I can't explain it, but shit just wasn't adding up, and it was getting worse day by day. I knew I had to do something and quick. I pulled out my cellphone still checking my rearview and called Gabrielle's number. She answered on the second ring.

"What's up, chic?" she greeted.

"I need you and Pamela to meet me at my house now. Money just tried to kidnap me!" I yelled frantically.

It wasn't the fact that I was scared of him anymore. I learned very well how to protect myself from people like him, but I made myself a promise the night I finally escaped from him, that he would never touch me again, and today, he got close enough to put his hands on me. If it wasn't for the two men that intervened, there was no telling what Money was going to do to me, but I was sure it was nothing good.

Twenty minutes later, I pulled up in my driveway and was met by my team. I jumped out of the Range Rover "Meet me inside," I instructed them before hurrying in the house. As soon as I stepped inside the house, I could hear LA having a heated conversation with someone on the phone. I kicked off my shoes and proceeded to the huge living room area. A few minutes later, the crew came walking in with Gabrielle and Pamela in tow dressed in all black.

They both came and gave me a hug and asked if I was okay, and if I was hurt? I assured them I was okay.

"What do you mean is she okay? What happened?" LA asked abruptly and ended his call. I swear I didn't want nobody else to get hurt, so I had tried my best to keep certain things away from the crew and LA, but shit had just gotten real, and it was time for me to let them know who and what we were up against. Money was not an ordinary street nigga; he was Jamaican and as ruthless as they came.

"Listen, I need everyone's attention. We got problems in the streets. Today, I was almost kidnapped by a dude I escaped from with the help of Montez," I stated.

LA and a couple of other members immediately started asking questions, but I cut them off quickly.

"We don't have time for all these side questions and rowdiness. I need to explain who this person is. His name is Money, he's from Atlanta, Georgia. He is the head of a sex trafficking ring and a big-time heroin dealer.

"If he got all that going on, why is he here in Cali?" Lil' trigger asked.

"According to Creep, he is the one trying to kill me, or should I say all of us," I informed them.

"Wait, something is not adding up, Jewelz. It's been seven years, and you had your name legally changed, how did he find you after all this time, and why does he want you dead?" Pamela asked suspiciously.

"I don't know why he waited so long, but you and Gabrielle both know that Money is not the kind of dude that you walk away from without consequences," I replied.

"Who else outside of the crew even knows your real name, and furthermore, about this organization?" LA asked causing everyone present to think hard.

Then the thought hit me and LA at the same damn time.

"Montana," we both blurted out simultaneously. The crew started to talk amongst themselves.

"Aye yo', Jewelz, you know all you have to do is give the order, and we on it. I don't care who these niggas are, they ain't fuckin' with us. We'll squad up," Big Mike said. I saw a few of them already on their phones making calls.

I walked to my room to gather my thoughts with Pamela and Gabrielle following behind me. If there were any women I trusted in this world, it was them, my Goon bitches. I knew that Money's only weakness was pussy, and that was where my girls would come into play. I was going to lure him in a trap. We set our plans into motion with a phone call and proceeded back into the living room with the guys.

I whispered my plans for Money to LA and then addressed the crew. "I got fifty-thousand for whoever can find Montana and bring him to the spot. I want his ass found now! Dismissed!"

# Other Books By Black Diamond

Inmate Love Affair